D0917022

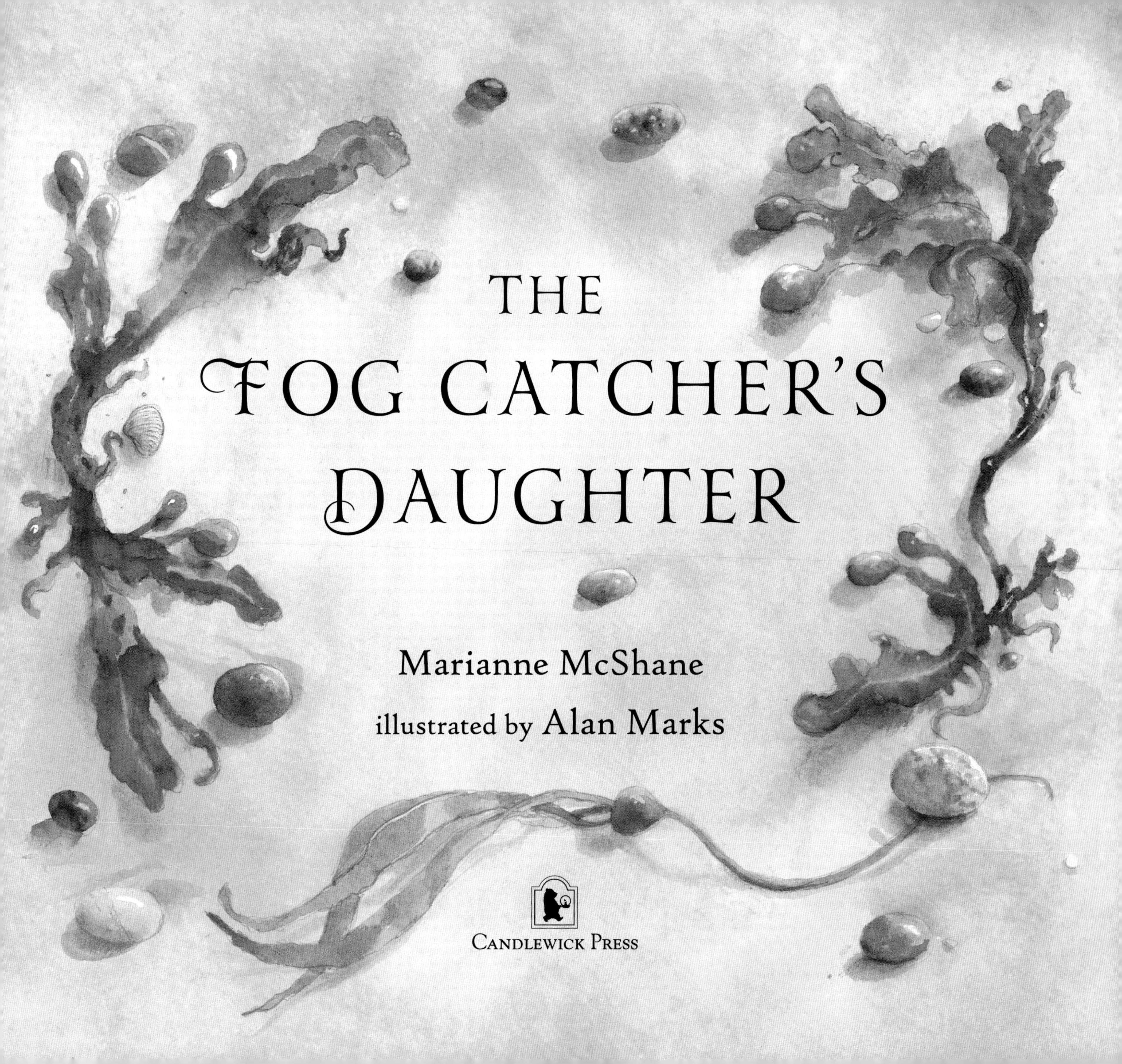

THE FOG CATCHER'S DAUGHTER

Marianne McShane

illustrated by Alan Marks

CANDLEWICK PRESS

There was a girl in Ireland. Eily was her name. She lived with her father the Fog Catcher in a little cottage three fields from the sea.

In the first field, they kept a brindled cow for sweet and creamy milk.

In the second field, they raised sheep with fleece as soft as sea foam.

In the third field, they grew herbs, sprinkled with magic fog water, that Wise Annie brewed into cures and braided into charms in her apothecary shop in the village.

One midsummer morning, Eily unlatched the half door and looked out at the isle of Lisnashee.

"It's the day for the crossing, Papa, isn't it?" she asked. Her voice was low and her heart heavy.

Lisnashee was no ordinary island. It belonged to the Good People, the fairy folk, and it was said to be enchanted. This was the day her father would tuck a charm for protection into his pocket, pack his nets, and row to the island to catch the magic beads of mist. Eily's family had been fog catchers for as long as anyone could remember.

Next year, it would be her time to go with him and learn his skills.

Everyone in the village kept well away from Lisnashee, for they dared not tempt the wrath of the Good People by trespassing on fairy ground. They knew there were unseen fairy paths even in their own fields. And they knew what could happen if they stepped on one. People spoke in hushed voices of cows that had stopped giving milk, currachs wrecked on the shore, and villagers themselves stolen away under the spell of the fairy sleep.

So they never let the sun rise without sprinkling a few drops of the Fog Catcher's magic water around their doors and windows for protection. And they never let the sun set without leaving a dish of freshly churned butter on the doorstep to please the Good People.

Eily and Papa set out that morning, her little hand slipped in his, to milk Molly, the brindled cow. Eily tossed the first few drops of milk into the air for the fairies as she always did. But this morning, she didn't sing her milking song to Molly. She called no greeting to the sheep. A shiver ran through her when she glanced out at the island. There was no fog yet, but the fairy wind was on the rise.

"Papa," she said back in the cottage as she mixed flour and buttermilk into soft cakes of wheaten bread, "there's a whole jar of fairy water left. Could we not make it last?"

Papa shook his head. "It'll barely last the winter, love, and we need Annie's cures and charms to keep away sickness and ill luck."

Eily bit her lip. She feared for her father rowing on those wild seas and getting caught in fairy spells on the island. But she knew that the Fog Catcher would not set foot on Lisnashee without one of Annie's charms in his pocket.

She dropped the wheaten cakes one by one onto the hissing griddle. At least she would make him good bread for the crossing. And perhaps she could find him a journey treasure.

After breakfast, Eily raced through the village to Annie's shop. She stepped into a fragrance of perfumes and potions. Annie was spooning ointments into jars. "What has you here so early, child?" she asked.

"To find a treasure for Papa."

"Take what pleases you best."

Eily looked around at the wonders and curiosities in the little shop—fleece and herbs entwined into charms, baskets of limpet shells and mermaids' purses, stones washed smooth as gulls' eggs. She saw a stone flecked brown and cream, the color of Molly the cow.

"This one, Annie!"

She tucked it in her pocket, and then she noticed that the creel by the door was empty. "You've used up all the seaweed, Annie. There's none left for the potions. I'll run down to the shore and fill the basket."

Eily had the creel nearly full when a cold wind shivered across the sand and the sky began to darken. Icy waves crept up the beach, biting her toes. Lisnashee was vanishing into the mist. She struggled back with the heavy creel, strands of seaweed trailing behind her.

"I have to give Papa his treasure, Annie.
The fairy wind is bringing the fog
to the island, and he must leave."

"A smooth way before you, child," said
Annie, sending her off with a blessing.

Eily reached the cove just as Papa was loading his nets into the currach. In a flurry of windswept hugs and farewells, she slipped the stone into his hand and then he was gone.

"Mind you leave out plenty of butter tonight," he called over the wind. "Shut the doors and windows tight."

And he rowed out to the fog.

Eily turned homeward. Stray tufts of fleece, tossed by the wind, fluttered in the hedgerows like white hawthorn blossoms. But one was unlike the others. Small glass beads were woven through the white. It was Papa's charm, snatched out of his pocket by the fairy wind.

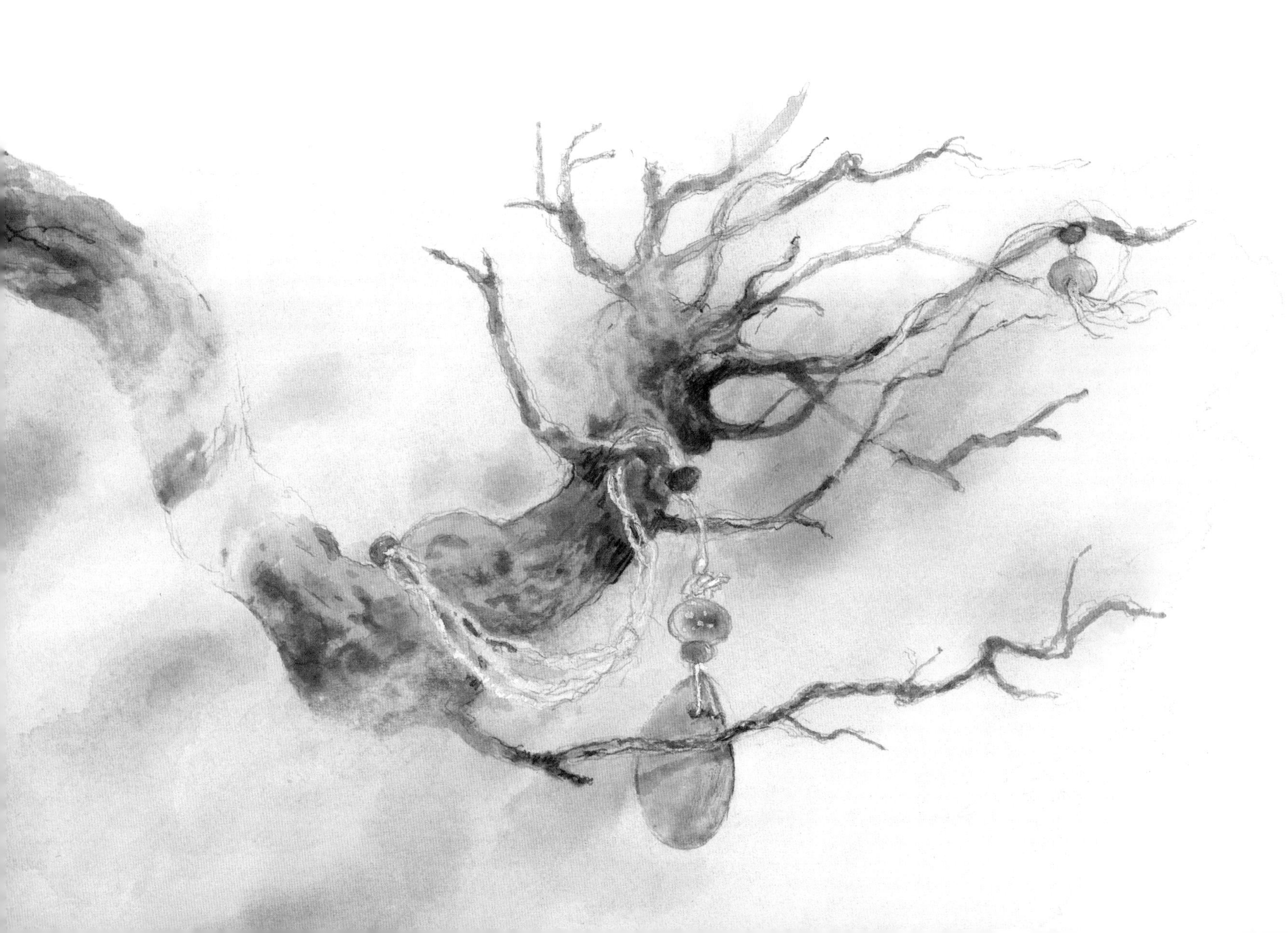

"Oh, Papa, how will you stay safe?" She untangled the charm from the hedge. *I'll leave the fairies extra butter,* she thought. *Maybe they'll do him no harm.*

Eily ran home so fast, she nearly outstripped the wind. She dragged Papa's chair over to the dresser, climbed up to reach the good china bowl, filled it with butter, and set it on the doorstep.

Then she curled up in the chair with the charm clenched tight in her fist.

It wasn't long before she heard a shrieking and a cackling above the wind. The windows shook and the door creaked on its hinges. There was a loud clatter—a breaking, a smashing. Then the wind died away. All was quiet.

Eily tiptoed to the door and peered out. The butter was smeared all over the doorstep, and the good china bowl lay shattered.

She stared at her father's charm and thought of him on Lisnashee without it. For a moment, she stood still. Then she shook her fist at the sky. She raced to the shore where the little boat her father had made for her just this winter was tied up. She rowed *Lapwing* out of their snug cove for the first time and into the storm-tossed sea.

Lapwing

The wind rose high and the current raged strong, but Eily took courage. She gripped the oars and pulled with all her might. Waves towered above the little boat, but Eily rowed steadily and *Lapwing* skimmed over the top of them. The village grew farther and farther away as she neared the fairy isle. She was almost there. But then *Lapwing* began to move in circles, spinning faster and faster. She was caught in a whirlpool.

Lapwing

She remembered Annie's blessing and chanted, "*A smooth way before me, a smooth way before me.*"

And sure enough, the little boat righted its course. *Lapwing* plowed through the waves to Lisnashee, and Eily clambered ashore.

Tendrils of fog coiled around her like cold damp cobwebs. She stumbled over the wreck of a boat. It was Papa's currach, smashed by the fairies.

"Papa!" she called into the storm. "I have the charm. I have a blessing. I'll bring you home."

At first she heard nothing. Then came a soft moaning. She followed the faint sighs and found Papa sprawled on the sand, drifting into the fairy sleep. She took his hand and twined the charm through his fingers. He opened his eyes and stared at her as if in a dream.

"Eily? Who brought you here?"

"I brought myself. In *Lapwing*."

He gazed long at her as if returning from far away.

She helped him to his feet, and he led her to a hollow in the sand where two jars of fairy water were safely hidden. She slipped her hand in his, and they carried the jars of precious liquid down to the water's edge where *Lapwing* was waiting.

Papa climbed into the little boat and stowed the water jars in the bow. Eily dipped the oars into the waves and guided *Lapwing* toward the shore where their little cottage waited, three fields from the sea.

"You'll make a grand fog catcher, Eily,"
said Papa. "You've no fear now."

AUTHOR'S NOTE

There are many islands around the coast of Ireland, although the Fairy Isle of Lisnashee is not one of them. It exists only in my imagination. But if you walk the coastline near the small town of Donaghadee, in County Down, you can gaze out at the tiny island that inspired my story of Eily and her Fog Catcher father.

The three Copeland Islands lie just over two miles from shore. The main island is so close that you can see the little white cottages on it. Some days the island glitters like a jewel in the Irish Sea. Some days it hides like a shadow behind the mist. I knew that one day I would write a story about it, but I wasn't quite sure what the story would be.

And then I came across an article about fog catchers who work in the desert regions of Morocco. For there are indeed fog catchers in the world! They make water out of thin air by catching tiny droplets of fog in fine mesh nets. Now I had my story.

As for the fairies—all over Ireland the folk belief in the Good People remains strong, and those who are wise take care not to offend them. You will often see a lone fairy tree in the middle of a field, for no one would be foolish enough to cut it down, and many farmers still toss the first drops of milk into the air for the Good People, just as Eily does on a midsummer morning.

For Tim, who traveled to the fields by the sea with me
MM

For Maya
AM

First edition 2022

Library of Congress Catalog Card Number pending
ISBN 978-1-5362-1130-6

22 23 24 25 26 27 APS 10 9 8 7 6 5 4 3 2 1

Printed in Humen, Dongguan, China

This book was typeset in Hightower.
The illustrations were done in watercolor.

Candlewick Press
99 Dover Street
Somerville, Massachusetts 02144

www.candlewick.com